TREASURES

TRACY MC CLURG

DEDICATION

For beautiful Neive who loves

searching for treasures

Treasures is an adventure that lets
you discover along the way.

It's your Treasure Hunt
So where you see a
⭐read your child/
Children's name/s.

Where you see a ❤️ read
The name/s of family or friends.

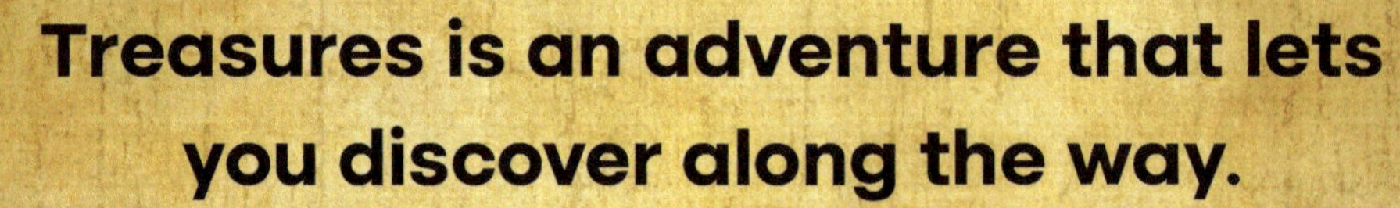

Treasures is an adventure for your small people to learn about who their family and friends are.

To help them imagine their favourite people when they can't be near – make a Treasures photo album in your device and save all the great pics of your family & friends that make you smile.

When you come to the end of the story, you can then have fun looking at the pictures together, supporting little minds as they make a connection with the people who love them.

Alfie & Mij love fun and adventures.
They love being outdoors and digging up treasures.

Take a walk with them and discover some treasures of your own.

Alfie and Mij love fun and adventures,
and their favourite game is
hunting for treasures.

Let's go find ⭐
to help with our quest,
to find gold, gems and rubies
for our dog's treasure chest.

They find ♥
in a field wearing wellies.
Singing whilst digging for
bright golden pennies.

We are hunting for treasure
and singing out loud.
Looking high in the trees,
and low down in the ground.

Shhh... don't make a sound...
We can hear ribbet, ribbet.
There's a frog for ⭐'s treasure chest.

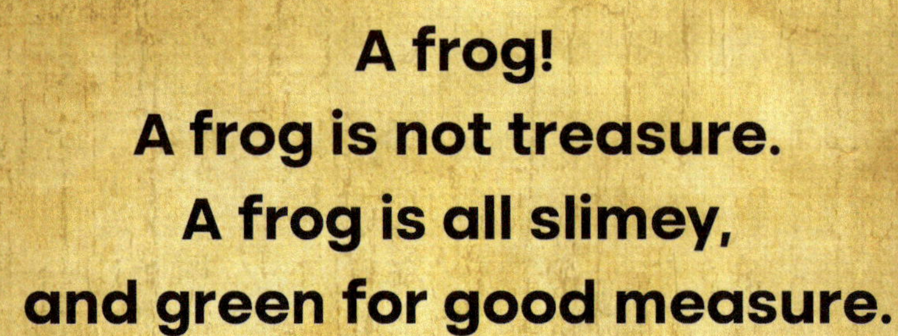

A frog!
A frog is not treasure.
A frog is all slimey,
and green for good measure.

It's not shiny like gold,
or bright ruby red.
We must travel on further
to find treasure instead.

Then they find ❤️
who's been playing for hours.
Looking for rubies in a garden of flowers.

We are hunting for treasure
and singing out loud.
Looking high in the trees,
and low down in the ground.

Shhh... don't make a sound...
We can hear buzz, buzz.
There's a bee for ⭐'s treasure chest.

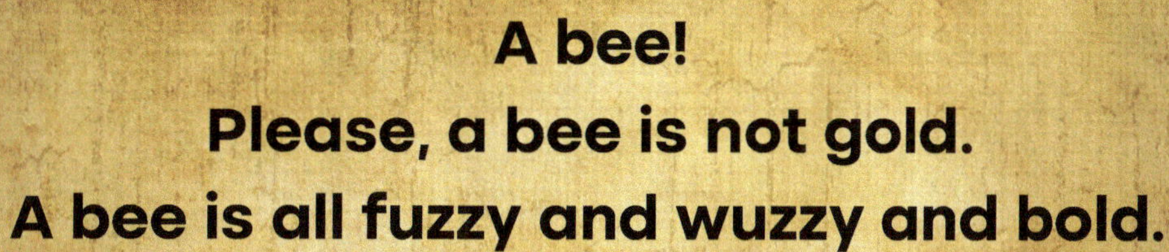

A bee!
Please, a bee is not gold.
A bee is all fuzzy and wuzzy and bold.

It's not shiny like gold,
or bright ruby red.
We must travel on further
to find treasure instead.

Then they find ❤️
in a forest of trees.
Digging for sapphires
under crunchy brown leaves.

We are hunting for treasure
and singing out loud.
Looking high in the trees,
and low down in the ground.

Shhh... don't make a sound...
We can hear cheep, cheep.
There's a bird for ⭐'s treasure chest.

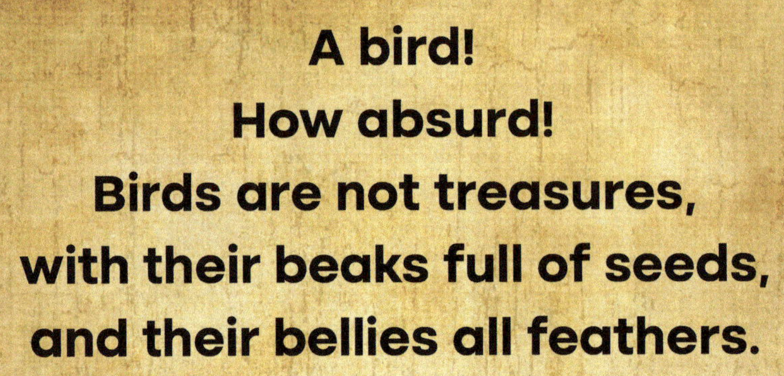

A bird!
How absurd!
Birds are not treasures,
with their beaks full of seeds,
and their bellies all feathers.

They're not shiny like gold,
or bright ruby red.
We must travel on further
to find treasure instead.

Soon they find ❤️
down by the sea.
Looking for diamonds...
1.....2.....3.....

We are hunting for treasure
and singing out loud.
Looking high in the trees,
and low down in the ground.

Shhh... don't make a sound...
We can hear mooooooo.
There's a cow for ⭐'s treasure chest.

A cow!
Wow, a cow is not treasure,
with horns and long tails,
and big mouths that do blether.

It's not shiny like gold,
or bright ruby red.
We must travel on further
to find treasure instead.

At the end of the road,
they find ❤️ ❤️ and friends.
They're all searching and looking,
to help ⭐ find some gems.

⭐ 's found frogs, bees and birds
and a cow that says mooooo
and while looking for treasure
found family too.

So this is where our big treasure hunt ends.
We've discovered the real treasure.....
is our family and friends.

THE END

AUTHOR BIO

Tracy Mc Clurg lives in Scotland and loves to write about all sorts of things - Treasure hunting dogs, Rooks with big beaks and adventures on the moon. Her mission - to make reading a special event in everyone's day. She is an author who feels that storytelling, above all else, should be fun. Tracy hopes that whether you are the one who is reading out loud or you are the small listener, you will always find ways to use your silly voices, sing and discover actions together that will bring her tales to life. Treasures is her debut picture book.

www.ingramcontent.com/pod-product-compliance
Lightning Source LLC
Chambersburg PA
CBHW042136120726
47911CB00022B/103